Hello, Neighbor!

Written by Michael Gaulden

Illustrated by Rod Flower

WiDō Publishing
Salt Lake City, Utah

Also by Michael Gaulden

My Way Home

WiDō Publishing
Salt Lake City, Utah
widopublishing.com

Copyright © 2023 by Michael Glauden and Rod Flower

All rights reserved. No part of this book may be reproduced or transmitted in any form or by any means, electronic or mechanical, including photocopying, recording, or by any information storage and retrieval system without the written consent of the publisher.

This book is a work of fiction. Names, characters, places, organizations and incidents either are products of the author's imagination or are used fictitiously. Any resemblance to actual persons, living or dead, events or organizations is entirely coincidental.

Cover design by Rod Flower
Book design by Marny K. Parkin

ISBN 978-1-947966-69-7

Dedicated to the beloved Marie Tuthill.
May her light shine within our spirits. Thank you for walking with us.

Well, hello there, I'm your friendly neighbor! My friends and family call me Harry.

Why do I sleep on sidewalks, you may ask?

Mostly, being hungry's the toughest part.
Sometimes good cats can have the roughest start.

Mr. Salem couldn't care for himself,
No litter of his own, to ask for help.

My friend, Mr. Tom, lives out here, like me,
Unemployed since they closed the factory,
A veteran who served our great country.

Kitty Kate never had a mom or dad,
A life as a stray was all that she had.

Mrs. Sabrina had a loving spouse,
But one sad day fire took more than her house.

At times some cats point, stare, or even yell, but everyone has a tale to tell.

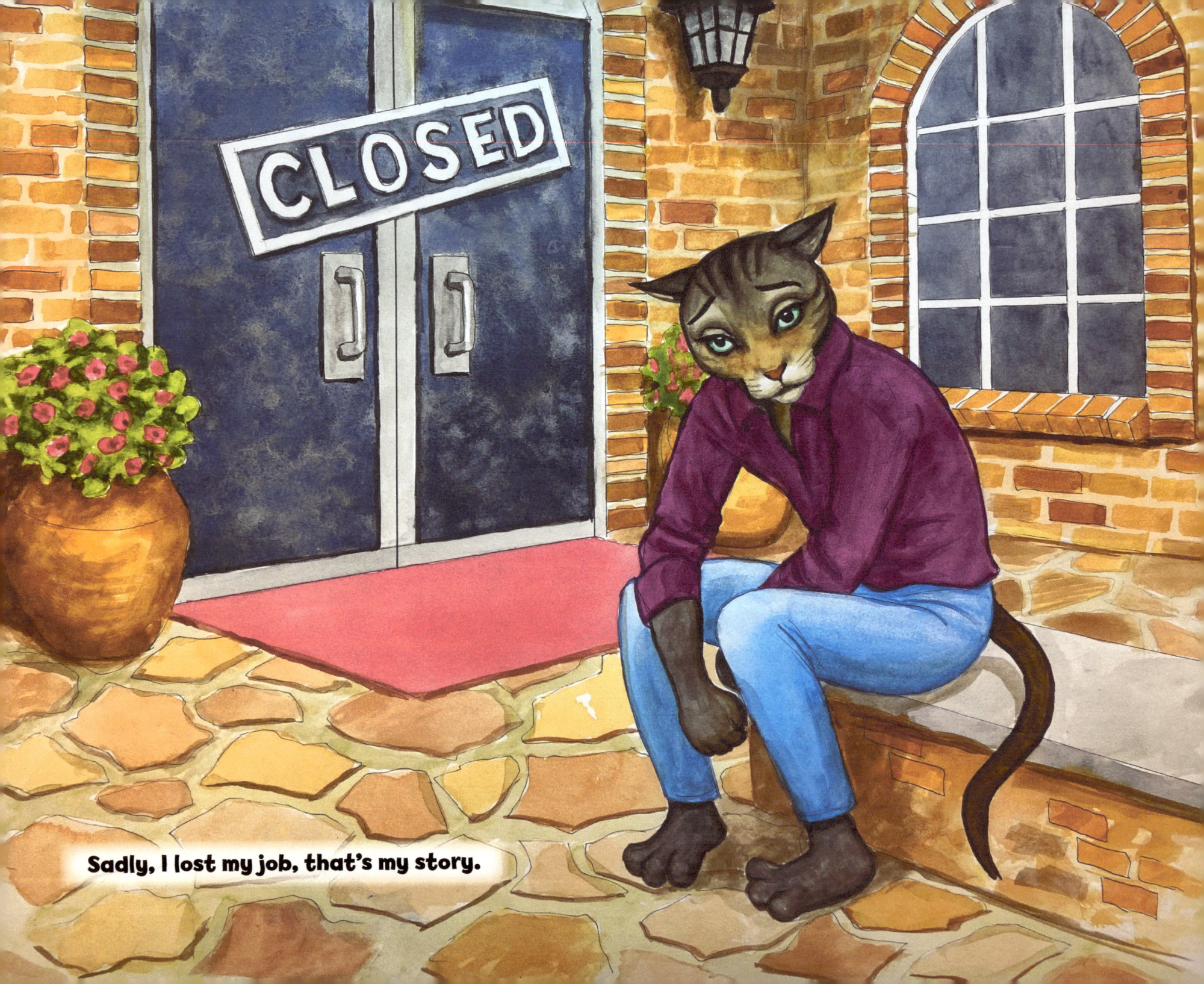
Sadly, I lost my job, that's my story.

I used to cook for fancy eateries,

And I will again one day, guaranteed!

Remember, if your tale gets in a twist, there are good cats around who can assist.

You see, my new friend, we're never alone,

And one day I'll find a home of my own.

Acknowledgements

As always, I send a special thank you to my incredible mother Monique Gaulden. Without her love and sacrifices, we would have never survived our own homeless journey. This book is dedicated to Marie Tuthill, a true wonder woman, force of nature, and loving mentor. Thank you for the guidance and for the laughs. You are loved and truly missed by our entire community. I want to give roses to Bobbi Spinner-Flack and Melissa Blackburn-Joniaux who are two of the most brilliant and inspiring women I have ever met. Thank you for your friendship and for all of your great work in the community.

About the Author

Michael Gaulden received his Bachelor of Arts degree from the University of California, Los Angeles. He is a former qualitative and quantitative researcher for UCLA. Gaulden is an advocate for the unhoused, foster care, juvenile courts, and all disadvantaged people. Gaulden is a professional public speaker who has spoken to thousands of audience members and multitudes of service clubs, schools and organizations. He is the author of *My Way Home*, a memoir that chronicles growing up homeless in the inner-city from ages seven to seventeen.

About the Illustrator

After receiving his degree from Oregon College of Art, **Rod Flower** embarked on a career as both a Fine and commercial artist. His work has included gallery art and commissioned portraiture, murals, landscapes and illustrations; as well as numerous theatrical productions as a scenic designer/artist. His artworks range from drawings to paintings to sculptures in EPS foam, with many projects combining 2D and 3D elements. Since 2018, he has been on staff as an artist/designer for a Houston Church. Currently Mr. Flower resides with his wife Adriana in the Houston area. This book is dedicated to Adriana, my best friend and the love of my life.

Printed in the USA
CPSIA information can be obtained
at www.ICGtesting.com
LVHW060800261023

762056LV00006BA/9